THE LONG ISLAND

for dana

Library of Congress Cataloging-in-Publication Data available.

ISBN 978-1-4521-5485-5

Manufactured in China.

The illustrations in this book were rendered in crayon.

10 9 8 7 6 5 4 3 2 1

Chronicle Books LLC
680 Second Street
San Francisco, California 94107

Chronicle Books—we see things differently.
Become part of our community at www.chroniclekids.com.

THE LONG ISLAND

DREW BECKMEYER

chronicle books · san francisco

They would sit and wonder about
the other side of the island,

and they would ride out

to see the far side.

The one too rocky
to land on.

The one too dense

The one
nobody
had ever
seen.

"We could go over it."

"Like with a bridge?"

"No. Like with a slide."

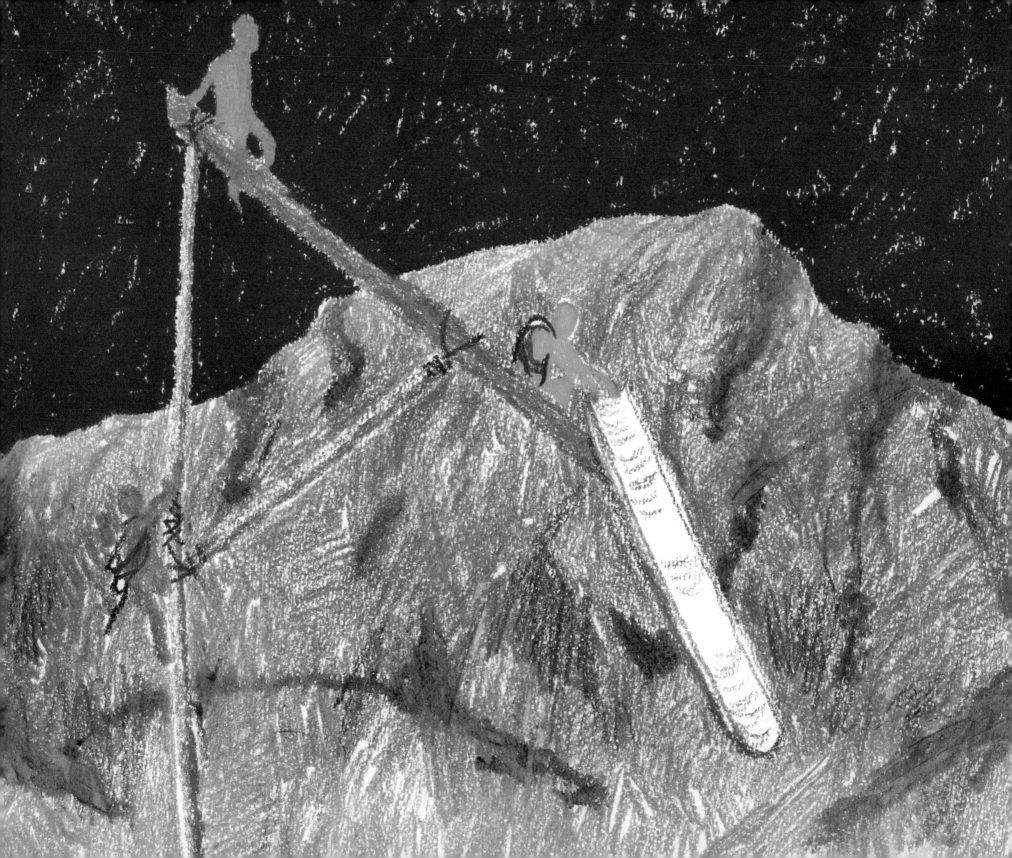

They did not stop

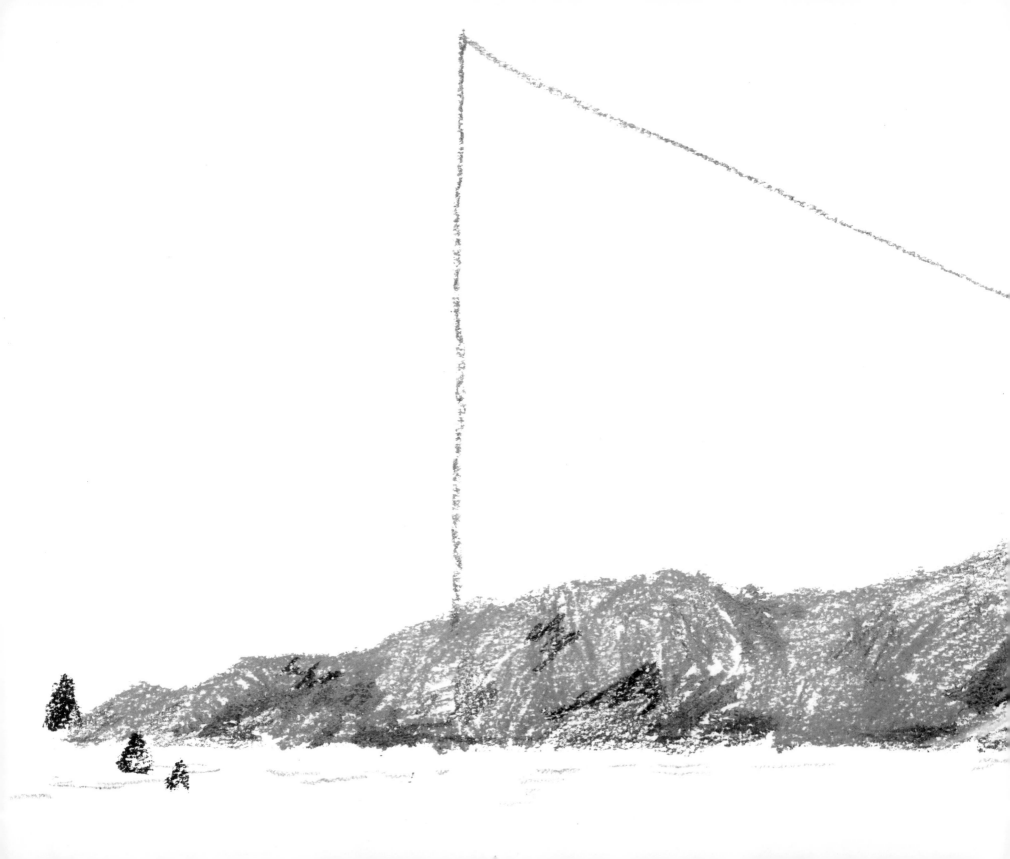

until
they decided it
was done.

And then they slid.

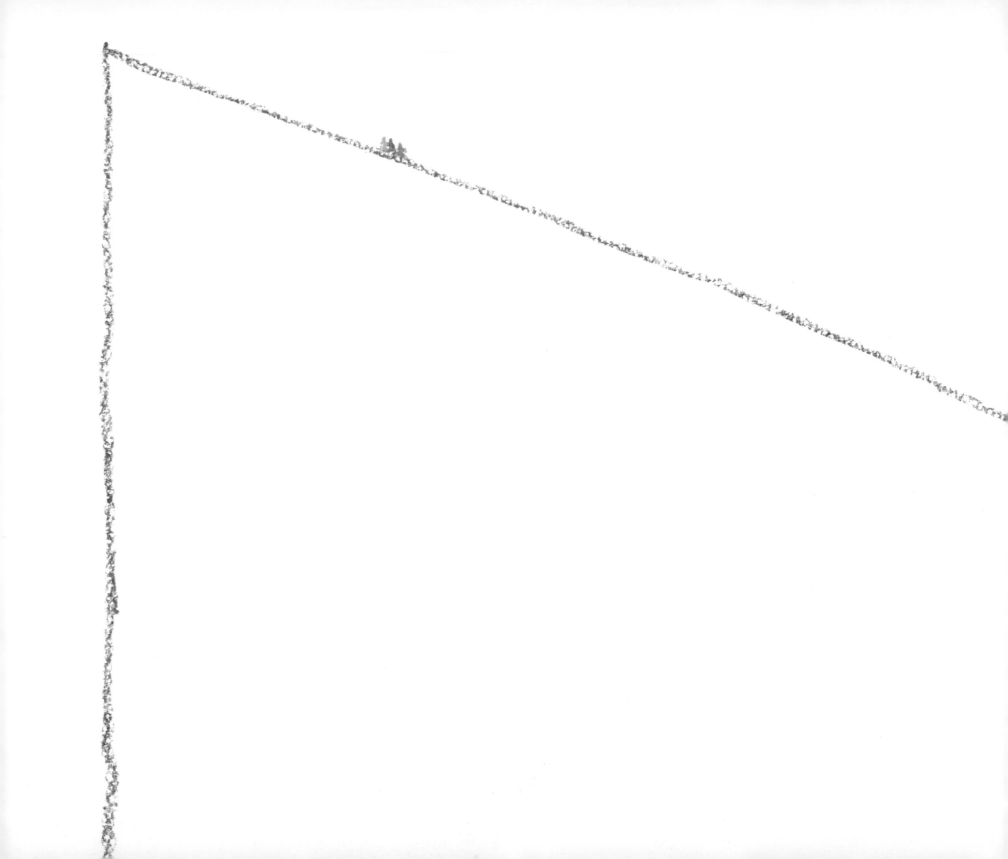

"We have been sliding forever."

"Whoa!"
"Whoa!"
"Argh!"

How do we get back?"

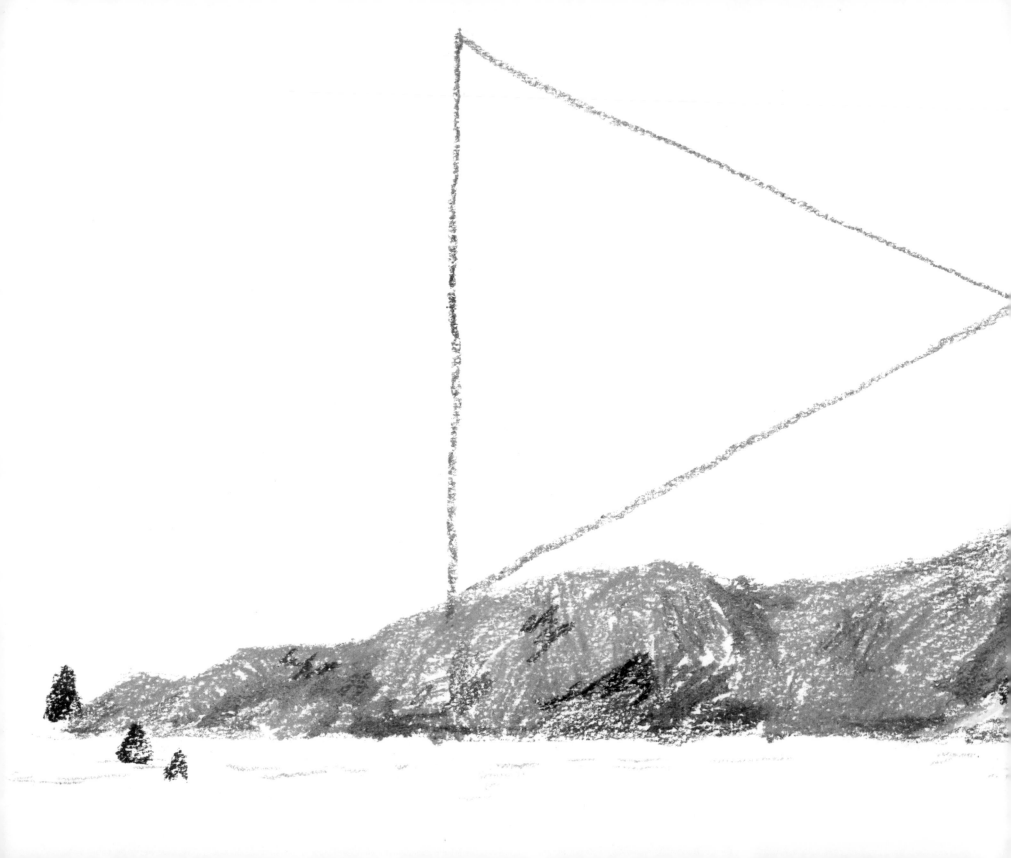

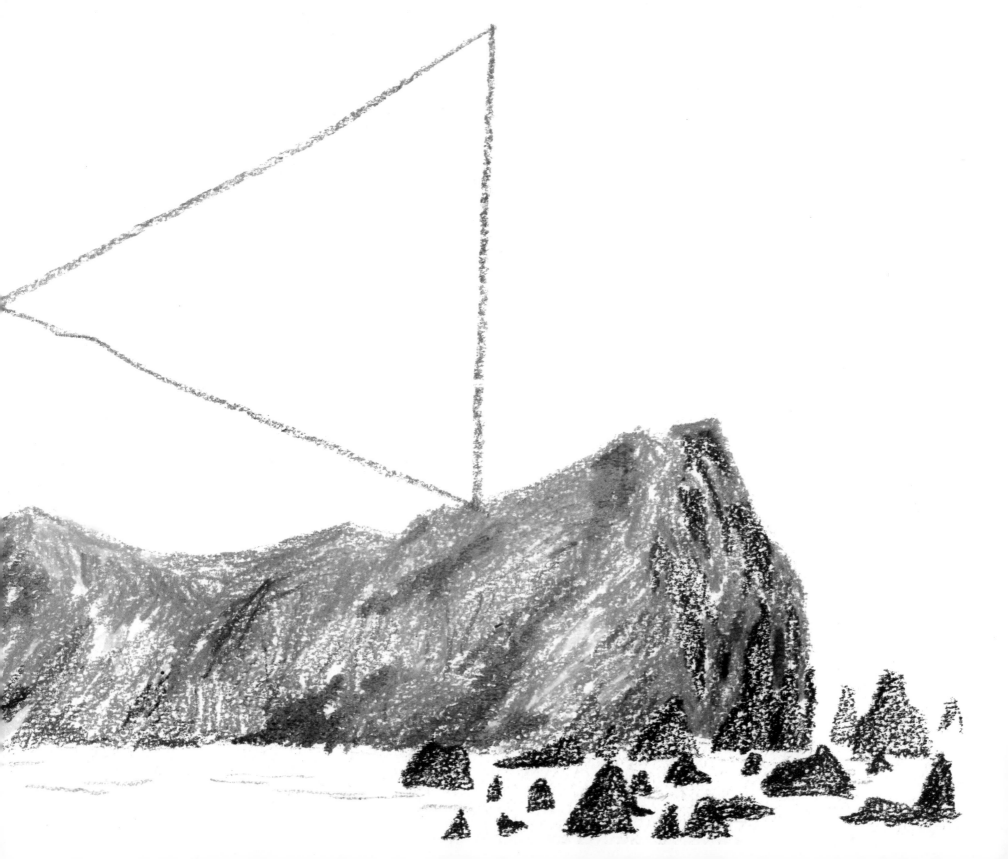

"How about
a tower
and
some other things
so we can see
if anyone
is coming?"

It was only a matter of time.

He would ride out
to find the place.

The one
too rocky
to land on,

too dense to
cut through.

The one nobody

had ever seen.